Hello, Family Members,

Learning to read is one of the m̶o̶s̶t̶ ̶i̶m̶p̶o̶r̶t̶a̶n̶t̶ ̶a̶c̶c̶o̶m̶plishments of early childhood. **Hello Rea**̶d̶e̶r̶ ̶b̶o̶o̶k̶s̶ ̶t̶o̶ help children become skilled reader̶s̶.̶ ̶B̶e̶g̶i̶n̶ning readers learn to read by remembering freq̶u̶e̶n̶t̶ ̶ words like "the," "is," and "and"; by using phonics skills to decode new words; and by interpreting picture and text clues. These books provide both the stories children enjoy and the structure they need to read fluently and independently. Here are suggestions for helping your child *before*, *during*, and *after* reading:

Before

- Look at the cover and pictures and have your child predict what the story is about.
- Read the story to your child.
- Encourage your child to chime in with familiar words and phrases.
- Echo read with your child by reading a line first and having your child read it after you do.

During

- Have your child think about a word he or she does not recognize right away. Provide hints such as "Let's see if we know the sounds" and "Have we read other words like this one?"
- Encourage your child to use phonics skills to sound out new words.
- Provide the word for your child when more assistance is needed so that he or she does not struggle and the experience of reading with you is a positive one.
- Encourage your child to have fun by reading with a lot of expression . . . like an actor!

After

- Have your child keep lists of interesting and favorite words.
- Encourage your child to read the books over and over again. Have him or her read to brothers, sisters, grandparents, and even teddy bears. Repeated readings develop confidence in young readers.
- Talk about the stories. Ask and answer questions. Share ideas about the funniest and most interesting characters and events in the stories.

I do hope that you and your child enjoy this book.

— Francie Alexander
Reading Specialist,
Scholastic's Instructional Publishing Group

If you have questions or comments about how children learn to read, please contact Francie Alexander at FrancieAl@aol.com

To Bob Wagner,
former and longtime Executive Director
of the American Zoological Association,
for his years of service;
and to the American Association of Zookeepers

—J.H.

To my parents, Frank and Betty Prebeg—
and brother Frank and sister Dana—
who put up with every kind of pet imaginable as I grew up!
And to my wife, Carole,
who wishes I could bring home every animal from the zoo!

—R.P.

Acknowledgments

Thanks to all the staff at the Columbus Zoo who helped make this book possible; to Rick Prebeg for his assistance with the book's content; special thanks to Sally South and Margaret Perry, who keep the busy office running while I'm on safari; Nancy Rose; J.R. Johnson, Kathryn Deyerle, and Spectrum Productions of our TV series, *Animal Adventures*; and to Diane Muldrow and Edie Weinberg for their great expertise!

—J.H.

Text copyright © 1998 by Jack Hanna.
Illustrations copyright © 1998 by Rick A. Prebeg/World Class Images.
Photographs pages 28 and 29 © and courtesy Michael W. Pogany, Columbus Zoo.
All rights reserved. Published by Scholastic Inc.
HELLO READER! and CARTWHEEL BOOKS and associated logos are trademarks and/or registered trademarks of Scholastic Inc.

JUNGLE JACK is a registered trademark of Jack Hanna. Used with permission.

Library of Congress Cataloging-in-Publication Data

Hanna, Jack.
    Jungle Jack Hanna's what zookeepers do / by Jack Hanna; photos by Rick A. Prebeg.
    p. cm.— (Hello reader! Level 4)
    "Cartwheel Books."
    Summary: Describes the work zookeepers do to care for various animals living in zoos.
    ISBN 0-590-67324-6
    1. Zookeepers—Juvenile literature. [1. Zookeepers. 2. Zoo animals. 3. Occupations.]
I. Prebeg, Rick A., ill. II. Title. III. Series.
QL76.H355   1998
636.088'9—dc21

97-32086
CIP
AC

10 9 8 7 6 5 4 3

9/9 0/0 01 02

Printed in the U.S.A. 23
First printing, April 1998

JUNGLE JACK HANNA'S
WHAT ZOO-KEEPERS DO

by Jack Hanna
Photos by Rick A. Prebeg

Hello Reader! — Level 4

SCHOLASTIC INC. **Cartwheel** B·O·O·K·S ®

New York Toronto London Auckland Sydney

Hello, Reader!

My name is Jack Hanna,
but lots of people call me Jungle Jack.
Ever since I was a little boy,
I have loved being around animals
big and small.
That's why I work in a zoo now.
The Columbus Zoo is a very busy place—
almost like a small city.
In this book, you will read about how
lots of people work to keep the zoo
a nice place for the animals.
Would you like to see what
the zookeepers do all day?
Let's go!

Early in the morning, before the visitors
arrive, zoo people are hard at work.
There are thousands of animals to feed,
and boy, are they hungry!
Most of the food for the animals comes
from a place called the *commissary*.
The commissary looks like a big kitchen.
Every morning, frozen meat is thawed.
Sweet potatoes and carrots
are cooked for the gorillas.
Fresh fruits and vegetables are
weighed and put in plastic tubs.

The tubs are delivered to animals all over the zoo.

Our eagle family eats ten rats and four trout every day.

Our lizards and frogs eat live crickets.

Our big cats, such as the tigers, eat ground meat six days a week.

On the seventh day, they are given bones to chew on. Bones are good for their teeth. And big cats do have bones in the wild.

Alicia has just prepared this reptile breakfast. *Yum!*

Juneau the moose's
breakfast has
just come from
the commissary.
He usually eats
grain and tree bark,
but sometimes he
gets a treat.
This morning
Juneau had a
banana.
Tomorrow he will
get a carrot.

Now that it's springtime, Juneau is shedding his hair — lots of hair. "It's time for the rake," says Kelly. Kelly uses a rake like a giant comb to help Juneau get rid of all that winter hair.
If you get a pet, make sure it is not a moose!

This morning Scott has taken a few branches from a maple tree for the bison. The tender twigs and leaves that the animals eat is called *browse.*

Most mornings, the bison eat grain—
as cows do.
The browse is a treat, a nice change from
the grain.

Would you like to take an elephant for a walk?
In the wild, elephants will often walk up to nine miles a day or more.

To keep our elephants from getting bored,
our keepers walk them outside every
morning before the zoo opens.
They guide the elephants by their ears
and say, "Go left" or "Go right."
The elephants understand them.
That's because the keepers spend a lot of
time feeding and caring for the elephants.
They trust their keepers.

Meet my old friend, Clyde the rhinoceros.
He lives in the same building as
the elephants.
Both elephants and rhinoceroses
are *pachyderms* (PACK-eh-durms).

"Pachyderm" means "thick-skinned."
Clyde's skin is so thick and so dry
that he needs to have oil rubbed into it.
Clyde is very big.
He needs a lot of oil!

This is Annaka.

He is a male lowland gorilla.

Annaka is twelve years old and weighs
375 pounds.

Annaka's keeper, Maureen, is training him
to follow her simple commands.

When Annaka follows the commands,
Maureen can take care of him more easily.

"Annaka, sit," says Maureen. He sits.

Maureen rewards him with food.

Annaka knows ten commands.

Some of them are Come, Sit, and Stand.

Now let's visit a very small gorilla.

Akanyi is a baby gorilla.
He is eight months old.
It's time for his
afternoon bottle.

Akanyi's mother was not able to care for
him properly. Keepers are with him
twenty-four hours a day.
Maureen acts like a gorilla mother.
She carries Akanyi on her back.
She naps with him on her chest.
She gives him lots of exercise.
She hugs Akanyi.
Akanyi hugs her back!

We want Akanyi to grow
up with other gorillas.
Every day, Maureen
takes Akanyi outside
to visit the grown-up
gorillas.
The female gorillas like
it when Akanyi visits
them.
They gather at the edge
of their habitat.
They put their arms
through the mesh
to try to touch Akanyi.
This is a good sign.
We hope that one of
the females will want to
adopt Akanyi when he
is old enough to move
into the gorilla habitat.

Let's walk over to the koala house.
It's time for Cindy to weigh the koala.
Minirri the koala walks to the scale
by himself.
His long nails click against the hard floor.
Minirri steps onto the scale.
Cindy says, "Today you weigh twenty-one
pounds."
That is a good amount for a koala
to weigh.
Minirri will probably go to sleep now.
He naps up to twenty hours a day.
When Minirri isn't sleeping, he is busy
eating eucalyptus (yoo-kuh-LIP-tus)
leaves.

In our nursery building, rhea (REE-ya) eggs are *incubating*.
They are being kept warm until they hatch.

A rhea egg is about the size of a grapefruit.

Every few days, Sheri weighs the eggs.

Do you see the numbers written on the eggs?

The numbers give the date we think the egg will hatch.

We have a lot of rhea eggs in our nursery.

When the eggs hatch, we will send the chicks to other zoos.

Many zoos want rheas.

These rheas hatched yesterday. They will soon grow to be five feet tall. Like ostriches, they do not fly.

There are lots of jobs to do in the zoo.
Cleaning is one of the biggest jobs.
Every day, cleaning enclosures and yards
takes up a lot of the zookeepers' time.
Jane is raking the cheetah's yard.
"Hello, String," says Jane.
She is not afraid of the cheetah.
That's because Jane has known String
since String was a cub.
String is used to having Jane in
the yard.

Our veterinary hospital is a very busy place! That's because most of our animals get regular checkups.

The vet staff takes a blood sample from a timber wolf.

A gorilla gets dental work done, along with a complete checkup.

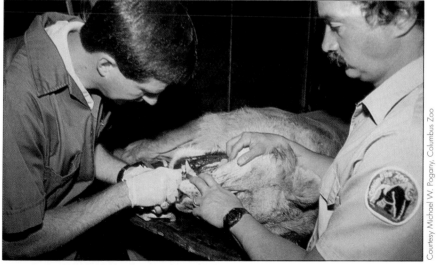

A lioness gets her teeth cleaned.

I love to visit our Discovery Reef.
It is a giant aquarium with corals,
fish, stingrays, and sea turtles.
Have you ever fed a stingray?
Paul does all the time!
The stingray swims to the top of
the tank.
Paul holds out a fish.
The stingray sucks the fish right
out of Paul's hand!

It's feeding time for the fish, too.
Every day, Lynn dives to the bottom
of the tank. She takes a bag of food
with her.
She hands the food to the fish.
Lynn makes sure that all
the fish get fed —
especially the ones that live on the
bottom of the tank.

Let's go outside and visit Kevin
and his birds.
Kevin takes care of many different birds.
Twice a day, the birds perform for zoo
visitors.
Kevin is getting the Andean condor ready
for the bird show.
This condor is only three months old.
His wingspan is six feet!
He will get much bigger!
His wingspan will grow to ten feet.

Condors can fly as high as 15,000 feet!
That's higher than some small
airplanes fly!
Warm air currents help lift the heavy
birds off the ground.
The timber wolves are watching
our condor.
I wonder what they think of this
big bird?
Let's visit some other big animals —
the giraffes.

The giraffe family has come inside
to have an afternoon snack of hay
and grain that Carl prepared.
The baby is six feet tall.
Her parents are fifteen feet tall.
Giraffes have the same number
of bones in their necks as
people do — seven.

Now let's visit some creepy, crawly critters!

Here we are in the *Arthropod* house.

Insects and spiders are arthropods.

Do you see the insect in the picture above?

It is on Jane's hand.

It is called a leaf insect.

Do you know why?

Jane is checking the health of this
walking stick insect.
She loves bugs as much as I do!
Now let's slither over to the reptile house.

Joel is moving this spitting cobra
from its enclosure into a bucket.
This is so Joel can clean
the snake's enclosure.
He uses a hook to gently lift the cobra.
He wears a mask to protect his eyes
from the snake's *venom.*
The venom is poisonous.
The cobra spits the venom out
of its mouth.
The cobras, below, live together in this
big box. They do not feel crowded.
In the wild, some kinds of snakes live
together in groups of up to 100!

This is a turtle egg.
To see if the turtle is growing normally,
the reptile keeper is *candling* the egg.
He shines a very bright light onto the egg.
Can you see the turtle inside?

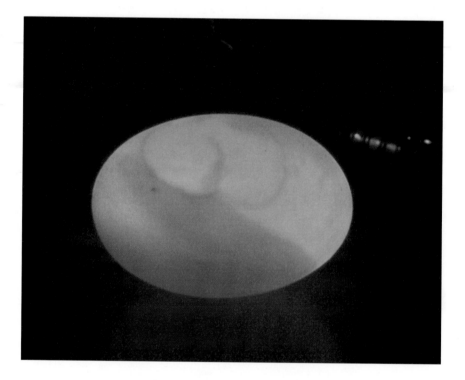

Another turtle is hatching right now!
The turtle uses its sharp egg tooth
to break open the egg.

The turtle is looking out of the egg
at its new world.
Here at the zoo, we are lucky to see
the beginning of many new lives.

Many more turtles have just hatched.
Liz feeds, cleans, and checks the health
of each turtle. Then she reports any
health problems to our veterinarian.
Let's leave the reptile house now,
and visit the animals that I take on
television shows.

These penguins are taking their vitamins, and they don't even know it.

Once a day, each penguin gets a vitamin pill. The pill has been put inside a fish. Jo hand-feeds the fish to the penguins. That way, we know that each penguin got his or her vitamins.

Hand-feeding our penguins also trains them to be friendly around people. That's important, because I take them on lots of public appearances and TV shows. Everyone loves penguins!

Today Suzi is letting the binturong
(BIN-too-rong) play all over her office!
This is how Suzi teaches him to be
friendly to people.
It's also a great way for him to exercise.
The binturong's tail is very strong.
It is used as a fifth leg to make
climbing easier.

This beautiful Persian leopard gets lots of exercise with Deb and Suzi.

I like to take leopards on TV. People do not get to see leopards very often. Leopards have become rare in the wild. Sometimes our frisky little Amur (uh-

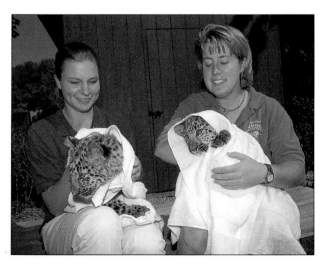

MORE) leopard cubs have to take baths after playing outside!

It is a big day at the eagle family's nest.
Kelly is taking the two chicks out of
the nest.
The chicks are eight weeks old.
They are almost old enough to live on
their own.
There are not many eagles left in our
forests, so these chicks will soon be
set free.

The chicks will be taken to
a forest.
They will live in a special
tower until they are used to
the smells, sights, and
sounds of the wild.
Then, on "release day," the
door to the tower will be
opened. The eaglets will be
free to fly away!

I hope you have enjoyed our day at the zoo.

You have seen more than most visitors get to see.

Maybe you will want to work with animals one day.

If you do, you will help other people learn about animals.

I think that's the best job there is!